A Spark of Reverie

Also by Suneé le Roux

The Reverie Flash Fiction Series

A Spark of Reverie
A Flight of Reverie
A Song of Reverie
A Whisper of Reverie

Standalone Short Stories

Spirit Caller

The Mythical Menagerie Series

Myth Hunter
Myth Keeper
Myth Maker
Myth Bringer

Keeper of Exotic Animals
Becoming Keeper

A SPARK OF REVERIE

A FANTASY FLASH FICTION COLLECTION

SUNEÉ LE ROUX

Strawberry Moon Press

Copyright © 2023 Suneé le Roux

Images prompted in Midjourney by Suneé le Roux.

ISBN (Paperback): 978-1-7764472-1-3

AUTHOR'S NOTE

Every month, as a special treat for my newsletter subscribers, I used to write a little flash fiction story - something that's very short (almost always under 1000 words, and at times even less than 500 words), and something that was sparked by my love of fantasy. The magic in these stories can range from the epic sword and sorcery kind, to the often overlooked magic that can turn a mundane situation into something a little more unusual. This collection contains some of these stories. I hope you enjoy them.

If you're new to flash fiction, might I suggest you read this book slowly. It's not meant to be devoured in one sitting. Give the stories a chance to breathe - I promise you'll appreciate them more this way!

This book makes use of UK English spelling and syntax.

TABLE OF CONTENTS

PENTHESILEA'S DEMISE

The clash of weapons reverberates through the air, humid and hot and heavy with the stench of sweat and blood and ash. A moan escapes the lips of the man before me and I pull my sword out of his stomach as his eyes glaze over, his gaze already drawn past the scorched walls of this great city and towards the Elysian fields, forsaking this mortal body with its gaping wound and its insides spilling out.

An arrow flies past my head. I duck instinctively and roll to avoid the stab of an enemy spear. I am back on my feet before the soldier recovers from his thrust. Surprise flickers across his face, perhaps only now noticing the curvature of my body underneath the boiled leather harness, or from the shock of my knife entering the exposed spot in his bronze breastplate and penetrating his armpit. I cannot tell. It doesn't matter. Blood gurgles from his mouth.

I move on. Death follows in my wake.

Just as I can no longer stand the stench, my mouth foul with the taste of rising bile and my hands spattered red, the wind changes and fresh air tickles across my face. For a moment, the carnage surrounding me diminishes as if it were an evil dream, and memories of home flash across my mind's eye.

Memories of the verdant steppes stretching out as far as the sun reaches, of riding bareback on powerful steeds, the wind whipping my long hair behind me. I see Themiscyra shining brightly in the moonlight reflecting off the calm waters of the lake beside it. I see hands stretched out in worship towards the goddess, moon mother, mother of all, life-giver. I see warriors training for battle. I see her, nodding with approval as my arrow hits its mark. I see her hand stretched out to me as she helps me to my feet again, my backside and my ego bruised by her prowess.

And then I see her, no longer a vision but flesh and blood, crumpling to the ground.

A scream rips the air apart, silence trailing behind it. My throat burns.

The world is me and her and the man who looms over her body. A tall warrior, gleaming in bronze armour, muscles slick with sweat, a red plume trailing from his helmet. A hero.

A monster.

He bends over her, his murderous hands remove her helmet. Blonde hair spills across her already-pale face. A smile plays across his lips.

White hot rage. A wordless roar.

The man looks up, startled, his eyes locking with mine.

Adrenaline pushes me forward.

He picks up a spear. Muscles ripple with the powerful throw.

The impact sends me sprawling.

I lie on my back, remembering the wind, the open sky, freedom. A beautiful woman's smile, a young man's obsession, and a wooden horse. So dies all that I hold dear.

The light fades. With my last breath, I turn my head to look at her. My fingers tremble as I try to reach for her, but my strength has fled.

Darkness overwhelms me.

ENDLESS LOVE

His arms burned from the exertion. He paused to wipe sweat from his brow, body long-accustomed to days spent out on the water automatically shifting weight as the little rowboat moved beneath him. The lake was restless. Its water reflected the dull grey sky above. Its water reflected his mood.

They were wrong, all of them.

Muscles bunched beneath his roughspun shirt as he heaved at the oars again. He had no destination to aim for. Somewhere between here and the far-off shore, she would find him. And she would prove them all wrong.

He just needed to keep moving.

As his limbs succumbed to the rhythm of rowing, his mind wandered to the woman who filled his dreams. Ethereal, beautiful, unattainable. They said she was a figment of his imagination. A vision conjured by loneliness, by a sun-addled mind searching for something he could never have. They said he was crazy. They said that if this woman existed, she would be the death of him.

They didn't know her like he did.

They haven't seen her face, pale in the moonlight, smiling sensually up at him. Her hair glistening like soft strands of spun silver. Her skin smooth and inviting. Her eyes fathomless like the deepest ocean.

He longed for her with every fibre of his being.

And then she was there, as if his thoughts had summoned her.

He barely heard the thump of the oars as they dropped into the boat. His bare feet scrabbled against the worn wood as he heaved forward, bending double over the gunnel. His fingers trailed through the water, like tears running down a cheek.

Her touch sent a shiver running up his arm. His eyes widened as her head broke the surface, water cascading down her flawless face. Her lips beckoned.

Fire consumed him as her kiss burned across his salty lips. His body ached with the need to envelop her in his arms. He wanted more. He needed more.

Her arms reached for him from the deep. They clutched at his body hungrily.

He went willingly.

The cold water closed over his head. Panic seared through his body as he gulped for air. His eyes burned as he struggled towards the fading light. Her clammy claws pressed into his skin, drawing blood. The fire in his belly turned to stone as his thrashing subsided. Blackness claimed him, her lips still on his.

They were right, all of them.

GHOST

S moke trails out of the back of the bus, so Miss
Edgar says we should all wait outside. The sky is
overcast and I don't worry too much about exposure
as I hop down the steps and join the others
clustering together towards the front. In our
matching grey jumpsuits, we mirror the bleakness
above.

Miss Edgar is yelling at the bus driver. The man
has disappeared head first into the smoking engine.
All I can see is his feet dangling while Miss Edgar
paces back and forth, her blue eyes blazing and her
scarlet dress getting filthier and filthier by the
second.

Our vehicle has broken down at a rest stop next
to the busy highway on the way to Lipsa City, but
there are very few other cars here. Probably why our
driver chose this place. From the edge of the
parking lot, I can see the gas station and a tuck shop.
Stunted trees are sporadic bursts of green beside the
dull grey tarmac.

It's my first Tour and my first time away from the
Compound. I've always wanted to see the Outside.

While Miss Edgar isn't looking, I slip away from
the group, ignoring their fading murmurs as the
wonders of the tuck shop beckons.

"Lida..." someone calls softly, but I pay no heed.

I pause outside the shop, peering through the
window. My breath quickens at the sight of so many
treats all in one place. There aren't enough years left
for me to earn this many rewards.

A thin ray of sunshine breaks through the

clouds, changing the light just enough so that the treasures inside are obscured by my reflection in the dirty window. There are no mirrors at the Compound, so it takes me a moment to realise that the face staring back at me is my own. My eyes are large and pale, my cheekbones high and my thin nose pointed. Straight white hair hangs down to my shoulders and my skin is so fair it's almost translucent. Just like the others.

"What are you looking at, freak?"

I turn around to see three girls confronting me. They are a riot of colours. Against my training, I can't look away.

"What's the matter, freak? Cat got your tongue?" the redhead asks, a sneer marring her beautifully freckled face.

The girl next to her sniggers. I wrench my gaze away from her blue painted lips and find no humour in her slanted kohl black eyes. Her hands are clenched inside the pockets of her purple leather pants.

The third girl smiles awkwardly at me. Her skin is so exquisitely brown I want to run my fingers along it just to see if it feels different too.

The redhead steps up to me and I tense as she slides her hand through my hair. "So soft," she coos, and then grips a handful and yanks my head downwards. I gasp as pain shoots through my scalp. She brings her lips close to my ear and whispers: "Never look your betters in the eye, Ghost."

"Leave her alone, Jess," the dark-skinned girl says and the redhead releases me. Then she shoves me and I stumble backwards, nearly tripping over the curb.

Heat rushes to my cheeks. I hear my trainer's voice in my head: *Never fight back*. Despite years of obedience, I can't help but glare at the girl before me now.

The girl with the blue lips chortles. "Looks like

our ghost has some fire inside her after all," she says. "Let's see if she wants to play." She pulls a penknife from her pocket. The blade flicks open, sunlight reflecting off its sharpened edge.

"Come on, guys," the ebony girl pleads. "Just leave her alone. She hasn't done anything."

"Of course she has," the redhead, Jess, says, her jade eyes cold as ice. "She exists."

That's my cue.

Before any of the girls can react, I launch myself into the air. I soar over their heads in a perfect front aerial flip, watching their eyes widen as my body rotates above them. I land lightly on my feet and sprint towards the nearest tree. My heart races as I scramble up its smooth trunk to one of the topmost branches. Out of reach. Safe.

"Come down and play, Ghost," Jess says in a sing-song voice. Goosebumps erupt all over my arms.

"There you are, Lida!"

Miss Edgar plants herself underneath the tree and frowns up at me. "Come down at once. We are ready to go." She turns towards the girls as I clamber down obediently and says: "Thank you for finding her. Lida is one of our most prized performers. I don't know what I would have done if something had happened to her." She hands a crisp blue note to Jess. "Thank you for keeping her safe."

Jess whoops in delight, and the three girls rush into the tuck shop without sparing me another glance.

I step into Miss Edgar's embrace. She hugs me tightly and I feel her body shaking. Her blue eyes search my face as she holds me out at arm's length.

"Are you all right, my dear?"

I nod, swallowing back rebel tears. "Why do they hate us?" I ask.

A sigh escapes Miss Edgar's lips, and her mouth purses into a thin line. "Because you're different."

I nod again, as if I understand.

"Come," Miss Edgar says, taking my hand. "Let's get back to the bus. The others are waiting."

I feel their grey-eyed gazes as I take my seat again. Avoiding their questioning looks, I turn my head and stare out the window. Jess and her friends are exiting the shop, their arms filled with bags of candy, their smiles wide and carefree.

Yes. I guess we are different.

But I am done being a ghost.

SKY PRINCESS

The princess times her ascent of the stepped pyramid perfectly, reaching its upper tier at the same time the sun-god is swallowed by the moon-demon. As the daylight dims, the crowd's ululating calls subside, leaving the hot, humid air as quiet as a graveyard. A trickle of sweat runs down the girl's temple, but her face betrays no emotion as the high priest, bedecked in black feathers and covered in river-mud, holds a hand out to her. Wordlessly, she steps onto the dais and lays down on the altar, staring up into the sky.

I have seen many sacrifices during my reign, but this is the first time the moon-demon's high priest has to restrain me. His cronies grip my arms tightly as I watch him prepare for the ritual.

The priest sways before the sacrifice like a jungle serpent teasing its prey. His bald head is drenched in sweat and only the whites of his bloodshot eyes are visible against the dark skin of his mud-smeared face. The curved knife, obsidian-black, seems to leech all light from around it, like a bottomless pit, a never-ending well of despair.

And still the girl does not move.

The sacrifice is necessary, I remind myself while I test the strength of my bonds. So we have been taught since the beginning of days. Once a year, we cast the names of our children to fate and once a year we watch one of them die. The moon-demon must be appeased. One life for the good of many. But never before has that one life been my daughter's.

The moment has come!

Quick as lightning, the knife shears towards the princess' heart. I roar, my arms bulging as fear races through my veins. My bonds hold.

A ray of light pierces the murk, illuminating the girl lying on the altar, untethered, unafraid. The priest hesitates, and in that moment, our hope is renewed.

The girl pushes herself up from the altar and, as she climbs to her feet, wings unfurl from her back. She stretches them to their full length, brown and powerful as a condor's. With one mighty beat, she launches herself into the air.

The ropes around my arms snap. The silence is broken. The crowd surges upwards, their thunderous voices joining my own, arms outstretched towards the newborn goddess. Their bodies trample the high-priest beneath them.

And as the sun-god breaks free from the moon-demon's bondage, I watch my daughter soar.

ASTERION'S ANGER

"Unacceptable!"

I slammed my fist on the table. Earthenware cups rattled as all eyes in the room turned towards me. My mother shook her head slightly, her hand resting on the king's arm. Daedalus, the king's advisor, narrowed his eyes as he studied me, as if I were a riddle to be solved. Lesser lords watched me the way a man watches a venomous snake.

"The agreement clearly states that Athens will send us seven young men and seven young maidens every seven years as a tribute," I said, feeling my frustration rise at their disapproving gazes. "Not three, not one, and certainly not none! If they cannot keep their end of the bargain, then we cannot keep ours."

"Agreed," the king replied, his voice a rough rumble. "But Athens has fallen on hard times. If we were seen to be lenient –"

"Don't be a fool, Minos!" I interrupted, ignoring the flash of anger that crossed my stepfather's face.

"Asterion..." Mother's tone held a warning. I paid her no heed.

"If we allow Athens to shirk their responsibilities, we will be seen as weak. It won't be long before we have an invading force in our own harbour."

"That might be true, but great leaders know when to show mercy." Minos' eyes bore into my own, his lips turned down in the ever-present scowl he reserved for me. Me, blond-haired and blue-eyed against his dark hair and olive skin. Me, clearly someone else's son. His resentment coated me like a layer of mud.

Heat rose within me. "How would you know?" I sneered.

Minos jumped to his feet. "Pasiphae! Take this bull-headed son of yours out of my council chambers."

A migraine exploded just above my eyebrows. "Bull-headed?" I shouted. "It's you who cannot be reasoned with!"

Pain blasted at each of my temples. I slapped my palms to my head and bellowed; from anger, frustration, or agony, I couldn't tell. Enraged, I grabbed my chair and smashed it on the table. People jumped to their feet, shouting.

Pain erupted from my forehead. It burst, like a melon impaled on a pike, exposing two curving horns, sharp enough to draw blood at my roving touch. My throbbing face elongated and I felt my ears stretching and drooping towards my suddenly shaggy cheeks. My vision blurred.

Movement caught my eye. I lowered my head and stormed towards it, hearing a satisfying scream cut short as I crunched into something soft.

"Restrain it!" someone shouted. The king.

Chains wrapped around my body. I roared, straining against my bonds. A cacophony of sounds surrounded me. I wanted to tear and rip and shred.

"Take it to the Labyrinth," a voice called. Daedalus.

"Asterion!" My mother's scream was shrill.

A sharp blow to the head. The world faded into blackness.

❧ ◆ ☙

The sun sparkles on the cerulean sea. A black-sailed ship glides into view. I watch it through a hole in the wall of my prison.

A smile flits across my bovine lips.

I turn back towards the darkness, into the endless twisting corridors of my new home. My horns brush against the low ceiling. I bellow in anticipation, a sound that echoes through the empty labyrinth, stirring cobwebs and dust, rattling old bones.

I have become what I had always seen reflected in the king's eyes. The thing he feared most.

I am a monster – and I am finally free.

Let the tribute come.

LINE 156

"Are you coming, Roy? Roy? Roy!" A face pops into my vision and I blink a few times, struggling to focus on anything other than the dimmed screen I've been staring at for the last few hours. It takes me a couple of seconds to recognise Eileen. Her face looks drawn, bleak. Too many late nights.

"Come on, Roy," she says, placing a hand on my shoulder. I try not to shrug it off. "Deadlines be damned. It's almost midnight."

"You go on," I say, breaking eye contact to adjust my glasses. "I've almost got it."

She takes a step back, huffing loudly. "Suit yourself."

I return my attention to the code, barely registering the office door slamming as Eileen leaves. I've been struggling with this bit of logic for hours now. No matter how many changes I make, how many times I run the query, the same red error pops up every time: OBJECT REFERENCE NOT SET TO AN INSTANCE OF AN OBJECT. It's driving me insane.

I press F5 and swear under my breath as the inevitable message is displayed again. A plague on the house of the developer who decided it was generic enough to use for every unexpected error.

The sound of a door opening and closing stops my cursing short. Eileen probably forgot something. I continue to stare at the screen as if, by some divine miracle, the issue would sort itself out.

A snicker breaks the silence. I look up, annoyed.

Surely she wouldn't be laughing at me... The room is dark, the light from my three monitors the only illumination. The only sound I hear is the quiet humming of my PC. I glance around. No sign of Eileen.

Probably a trick of the imagination.

I return to the code. Perhaps if I –

My head whips up as another maniacal giggle disturbs the peace. I scan the room. Suddenly the shadows seem ominous. My heart races as I perk my ears for the slightest unusual noise. My palms are sweaty as I return my fingers to my keyboard.

I sit frozen like this, poised to type. All is quiet. Maybe Eileen was right. Maybe it is time to call it a night. But I just need to fix this bloody –

The hair on my arms stands to attention as hot breath tickles across the back of my neck. I swallow audibly. I've seen my share of horror movies. I know how this ends.

"There's your mistake," a high-pitched voice announces. "Right there, line 156."

I exhale slowly, gathering courage. Then I look over my shoulder.

And nearly fall off my swivel chair.

The ... thing ... keeps peering at my monitor. Its large bulbous eyes reflect the faulty code, like a tarnished mirror. I flinch as it lifts its furry red arm, wafting the smell of week-old pizza and stale beer in my direction, and touches the screen.

"Right there," it says, looking at me. Its lips split in a monstrous grin, revealing pointed teeth that have bits of something green stuck in them. "Line 156."

I risk a glance at the spot where its clawed finger left a mark on my screen. As I inspect the code, I'm acutely aware of the monster standing beside me. I don't know what the green stuff in its teeth is, but I'm betting it's not lettuce. My body is taut with tension. Any minute now, the monster is going to take advantage of my distraction and pounce. I can still feel its hot breath on me...

Wait, what? Well, I'll be damned.

I add the missing semicolon to line 156. My hand trembles as it hovers over the F5 key. I bite my bottom lip as I press the key and watch the code run.

Success!

I whoop with joy and turn towards the monster, my hand lifted in a high five.

Empty space confronts me. The monster is gone.

I turn back towards the screen, heart beating furiously. It takes me two minutes to upload and commit the code. Another five to fill in the leave form.

Eileen was right. Deadlines be damned.

JADE'S STANCE

Jade's long black braid dropped to the ground as she kicked her body into the air, balancing on both hands. She closed her eyes, blocking out the sight of the white-topped mountain peaks, the evergreen trees around her, the river coursing past the rock on which she was perched. She exhaled loudly.

With her eyes closed, it was as if all her other senses were heightened. In the distance, the caw-caw-caw sounded of the family of blackjays that had made the top tier of the monastery's pagoda their summer home. The scent of wild hyssop wafted on the early morning air, and the icy spray of the river kissed her skin as it rushed past.

Focusing, she slowly lifted one arm off the rock. Her other arm trembled and, for a moment, her body wavered like a sapling in a spring breeze. She resisted the temptation to open her eyes. Inhaling, she turned her focus inwards, ignoring everything but her own breathing.

In, and out.

In, and out.

Her arm steadied. Her body stilled.

Perfect balance, perfect unity.

A shriek rent the air, and Jade's eyes shot open. Her legs swept down and her body twisted instinctively into a martial stance, arms spread, palms outward. Her eyes roved across her surroundings.

Nothing seemed out of place.

But admission into the Temple of the Silent Fist was granted at the cost of a vow of silence. Jade hadn't heard the sound of anyone's voice in ten years, since the day her parents had left her in the care of the armed monks. Her mother's whispered farewell, her father's soft promise of a better life; those were the last words she had heard spoken aloud.

She hesitated for another moment. The silence was deafening. Not even the birds dared call.

She launched herself off the rock, leaping across the river and onto the grassy bank. With fluid grace, she bent to retrieve her stave from where she had left it lying earlier. Her feet pounded across the moss-covered forest footpath. Her braid flowed behind her as trees sped past, a blur of green and russet shadows. Jade's stomach twisted as the monastery's fortressed walls came into view.

The great gate hung open, one door drooping askew.

Jade raced through the arch, her breathing loud in her ears as she stopped short in the sunlit courtyard.

It was empty.

On silent feet, she padded across the worn stones and into the cool darkness of the main hall. Marble floors and austere stone walls greeted her. Her head whipped from side to side as she searched the vacant room.

Where were they?

No apprentices practicing the forms, no masters wordlessly correcting their stances. No one meditating in private alcoves. No scholars studying ancient scrolls of wisdom. As Jade walked through the empty passageways of the monastery, up and down stairwells, past prayer rooms and private cells, empty kitchens, abandoned common-rooms, and finally reached the courtyard again, she could no longer deny the truth, inexplicable as it was.

She was completely alone.

Alone.

The silence, no longer the welcome friend she

had always taken for granted, wrapped oppressively around her shoulders, stifling, threatening, baffling.

"Hello?" Her voice was hoarse, unfamiliar in her ears. It sounded desperate, scared. The voice of a stranger. The sound of a broken vow.

"Hello."

Jade's gaze snapped towards the echo. The man's face was as familiar as her own. She drew in a ragged breath as his name caressed her lips.

Taigan.

A lifetime's memories assailed her. Two children, eyes large as they stare at each other across the unfamiliar room, their first day in the monastery. A boy, crying alone. A girl, touching the boy's shoulder, the same loneliness pools in her eyes. His smile, shy, as he shares the sweet treat she hadn't earned. Her laughter, suppressed behind calloused hands, delighting in a hidden trove of flowers. His touch, steadying as they practise stances together, a waterfall surging behind them like the exhilaration in her veins. Her gaze, as he meditates through movement, his body a poem in motion.

His eyes were hard as agates as he watched her now. In his hands, he held twin blades of forbidden steel. His voice, when he spoke, was as smooth as whispered dreams.

"Come with me."

Speech bruised her lips as they stumbled over the words. "What did you do?"

His smile, once warm, chilled her bones. In answer, he sheathed a blade and held a hand out to her. Beckoning.

Slowly, Jade exhaled. There was nothing else. Perfect balance and perfect unity.

Just him and her.

Her grip tightened around her stave.

LAST STAND

"When will they get here?" Vala asked, a line creasing her forehead as she watched the approaching ships on the horizon. The sun was barely in the sky, painting the frozen landscape in shades of pink and orange. Her breath frosted in the still air.

"An hour. Maybe two," Jorg replied, his gruff voice sounding rougher than usual. She glanced at him. He had braided his beard this morning and, like her, had painted Bear's sigils across his face in blue war-paint. Strength. Courage. Victory. They were going to need it today.

Vala clenched the haft of her axe. She would not let these invaders, these marauders, threaten her home. She would fight. Fear gripped her heart, like a noose around a hare's neck, but she buried it deep. She would fight, and she would triumph.

She could hear muted calls and the clink of metal behind her as the village prepared for the attack. Farmers, hunters and craftsmen, men and women alike, all were pulling on chain mail and sharpening steel. Vala's smile was grim. They would not find her village an easy target.

The warning had come in the early morning hours, when the sun still hid its face from the world. A lone survivor from the neighbouring village, three days' hard ride away, had collapsed, barefoot and bleeding, in front of the palisade gate. "They're coming," the boy had wheezed, shivering from cold and fear alike. He was in the longhouse now, recuperating. Vala hoped he survived. The lad was brave. His family, rest their souls, would have been proud.

Jorg swore loudly beside her and Vala felt the blood drain from her face. The wind had picked up, an unnatural gale suddenly blowing in from the tranquil ocean. The ships' sails billowed, the sleek vessels speeding towards the shore. At this rate, they would land within minutes.

"Sorcery," Vala breathed, the word bitter on her tongue. She pulled her gaze from the oncoming threat towards her village. They would not be ready in time.

The wind whipped her red braids around her face as she turned back towards the shore. She could see metal glinting in the pale sun. The ships' decks were already swarming with warriors. The gust carried their battle cries to her ears.

Her stomach twisted as she gripped her own weapon tighter, palms suddenly slick with sweat. She licked her lips. Soon, the snow would be stained red. Would her blood mix with that of her enemies? Would the skalds sing her praises after this day?

"Are you with me, Vala Valkyrie?" Jorg growled, unsheathing his sword. His eyes were hard as stone, cold as a winter's morning.

Vala bared her teeth in a snarl, her fear drowned by the blood pounding through her veins. She lifted her axe in the air and roared, her voice echoing across the plain in a wordless challenge.

"Let them come," she said.

INVADER

The grunts of the oarsmen filled Ulf's ears as he strode across the longship's deck, his hand resting on the shaft of the double-bladed axe strapped to his side. He stopped a few feet short of the ship's dragon-headed prow, loathe to get too close to the watcher waiting there.

The rising sun shimmered orange across the calm water. In the distance, on the snow-covered shore, two small figures could be seen, observing their approach. Ulf's fists clenched.

"We will not catch them unawares this time," he growled.

This village would be just like the others. No doubt their stores were full, their bountiful lands having provided enough food for the long winter months. The people would be fat, soft, wrapped up in furs against the cold. Their coffers would be lined with gold gleaned from trade with even richer lands to the south. While these people, these infidels, slept in their warm beds, his people starved. His people died.

A deep-throated laugh came from the woman standing at the prow. She had her back to him; her gaze cast out across the ocean towards the land. Goosebumps rose on Ulf's skin as the witch turned to face him, her black-rimmed eyes meeting his own. She had smeared her skin with ash and covered her body in Snake's black swirls. She lowered the twisted steel staff she carried until its sharpened end pressed against Ulf's throat.

He swallowed nervously, feeling the trickle of blood as its point parted his skin. A sharp metallic tang tinged the salty air.

"Do you doubt me?" Her voice was low, threatening. A bead of sweat formed on the nape of Ulf's neck.

Ulf swallowed again, his throat suddenly dry. "Of course not," he said. "But the sea is still, and they have seen us."

The witch retracted her staff, inspecting his blood on its end. It seemed unnaturally bright, crimson against her ghostly skin as she slowly wiped it off with one finger. Then she stuck that finger in her mouth, closing her eyes with relish. When she opened them again, her pupils were slit like a serpent's. The witch bared her teeth in a bloodstained snarl, thrusting her staff into the air.

Ulf took a step backwards as the sky tore apart. A gale ripped free, howling in a vortex around the witch. He braced himself against the wind while adrenaline rushed through his veins.

Victory would be theirs.

He staggered backwards as the witch's gaze swept upward, taking the wind with it. The sails snapped taut, billowing in the gale. Ulf's hand tightened against his axe's shaft as the longboat sped towards the shore.

"Arm yourselves," he roared over the raging wind and the oarsmen's cheers.

He turned his back towards the men as they scrambled for their weapons and watched the land approach. Soon the soft snow would churn in the rage of battle, streaked with blood and guts and gore. Soon, this village would burn, just like the rest.

He would take what he needed and kill what he didn't.

And then he could go home.

MELIA'S ESCAPE

M elia winced as leaves crackled underfoot. The forest was eerily quiet. Mist veiled the smooth white boughs of the towering birch trees, like a spider's web wrapped around tall sticks. A carpet of red leaves blanketed the ground, crimson droplets on the barren earth.

A sound shattered the stillness. A hound barking.

Melia's head snapped towards the noise, her heart thumping in her chest. There! A beam of sunlight burned through the fog, clawing towards her.

She ran.

Heedless of the noise her feet made, or of the blood-scent she left behind as a stray branch scored her pale cheek, she ran. Her heartbeat drummed in her ears, her breath was ragged. Pain seared through her lungs.

The light hunted her.

Gasping for air, Melia stopped, a hand clutched to her side. There was nowhere to go. A sheer cliff rose up before her, its jagged rocks slippery and unassailable. She turned, pressing her back up against the wall.

Two hounds burst from the mist, their lithe, muscled bodies eager to tear, to rip. They confronted their prey.

Melia was not afraid of them.

Her breath caught as the light drew closer. Already, the mist was fading, white turning to yellow, the sky appeared overhead.

Dizziness assailed her. Her whole body

trembled. She closed her eyes against the brightness.

And... stretched.

Her body elongated, her feet dug into the cool earth, her arms extended into the sky. Clothes fell away from the tall trunk that had once been her fragile figure. Leaves sprouted from limbs that had once been flesh. A breeze swished gently through the foliage that had once been her lustrous hair.

Wind wrapped around her, a soft exhale, a sigh of relief.

A tall man stood below her. Golden hair shone in the sunlight that oozed from every pore of his powerful body. He whistled and the hounds lay down at his feet.

The man placed a hand on her trunk. His touch sent a shiver through her. Her leaves rustled.

"Oh, Melia," the man sighed. "I did love you, you know."

He shook his head and turned his back on her. His footsteps tore red gauges into the earth, his hounds and the sunlight following in his wake.

Melia watched him go. Little. Insignificant.

She wrapped the returning fog around her, a cold, welcome blanket.

She was free.

NAIA'S PROTEST

"War? Are you out of your minds!" Naia's voice echoed through the chamber. She closed her eyes for a moment and breathed in deeply. When she opened them again, the faces of the Twelve frowned down at her from their raised seats.

"You forget your place, Priestess," the First said, his deep voice rumbling through the marbled hall.

"No, your forget yours," Naia immediately countered. His look of disapproval only inflamed her rage more. "Do we serve Ares now?" she demanded.

"Our conquest will bring honour to Poseidon. We will make Atlantis great again."

Naia's mouth fell open. She glared at the old men gathered in front of her, a semi-circle of the island's most powerful speakers. Elected in their youth, they were supposed to be their nation's protectors. They were supposed to serve alongside her.

The years must have addled their minds, Naia decided. Is this what comfort and greed and pride do to men? Could they really believe that aggression would solve all their problems? That the death of thousands, the loss of family and homes, the razing of the land, that all of this would be an acceptable tribute to the god of the oceans?

"You will bring about the downfall of Atlantis."

The hair on Naia's arms stood on end as the Prophecy lingered in the air, the truth of her words ringing in her ears.

Shocked faces mirrored her own and suddenly

everyone was speaking at once, but the First's voice dwarfed all others. "Remove the heretic. Her words bring only contention."

Strong hands clasped her arms, but Naia shrugged them off, scowling at the guard. The man retreated from the fire in her eyes. Without sparing the Twelve another glance, she turned her back on them and strode out of the council hall.

She paused as she reached the pillared steps leading down towards the city. Naia's gaze wandered across her home: the concentric rings leading outward from the palace and the temple down below, white stone buildings shining like beacons in the bright sunlight, water from the canals gleaming gold on blue. Her eyes swept towards the harbour, where thousands of ships lay anchored, their silver sails billowing in the breeze.

The wind chilled her bones.

Then the earth rumbled.

Naia stumbled, clutching at the trembling pillar beside her. She ducked as bits of debris rained down from the roof. It had gone dark all of a sudden. Naia looked up to see the sun shadowed, swallowed by a sphere of darkness.

Ignoring the shaking earth, she climbed to her feet. So soon? She needed to get to the temple. Perhaps there was still time to placate the gods.

A roar filled her ears. Her head whipped towards the sound, and her eyes widened. An enormous wave was rushing in from the sea. The ships in the harbour bobbed like a child's toys in its swell.

Fear shot through Naia's heart.

A teardrop rolled down the priestess' cheek. "Poseidon protect us," she breathed.

But it was too late.

THE LOST CITY

The goddess Zuraya was in a pickle.

Her hands trembled as she placed the scroll down on her desk and removed her glasses. She rubbed at her temple where a migraine was brewing. She inhaled deeply, trying to slow her rapidly beating heart – unsuccessfully.

Returning the spectacles to the bridge of her nose, she picked the scroll up again and continued reading the Pantheon's missive. Her palms grew sweatier the further she read. The letter contained words that made the pit of her stomach twist into knots. Words like "unacceptable dereliction of duty", "immediate resolution" and – she gasped – "personal onsite attention".

"They want me to go into the field!" she exclaimed, aghast.

She fluttered a hand next to her face, her cheeks suddenly flushed. A droplet of sweat rolled down her spine and settled uncomfortably on the small of her back. It had been ages – millennia! – since she'd last left the familiar confines of her quarters and the citadel at large. Expecting her to leave this haven, now of all times, to walk among mortals – and agnostic ones at that – was preposterous!

It wasn't her fault the city had been lost, after all. She couldn't be held responsible for what that man had done. She'd trusted him. She was the victim here.

The door to her office creaked open and Talira slipped in. "Is it true?" the young goddess asked, her face a mask of bewilderment. "The entire city of

Bravneem has been lost?"

Zuraya nodded, her shoulders slumping. She might be able to reason herself out of guilt, but there was no hiding anything from the goddess of truth.

"But how is this possible?" Talira exclaimed. "Bravneem is a Holy City! People flock there to worship us. How can it just disappear?"

"Vidhen." Zuraya felt unaccustomed heat rise in her cheeks at the sound of the man's name. She'd been a fool.

"The apostate?" Talira's brow furrowed. "How did he escape? Unless…" Her eyes widened and her mouth formed a surprised oh. "Zuraya!"

"It was the logical thing to do!" Zuraya said, jumping to her feet, her heels clacking as she paced the marble floor. "How best to convert a man devoid of faith than to surround him by the faithful?"

"If spending his days in our presence was not enough, how could liberating him from our guidance induce his allegiance?" Talira asked.

Zuraya hated when someone used logic against her. Reasoning was her domain, after all. But she had to admit, Talira had a point. And she could see now how Vidhen had manipulated her, too.

"My judgement was flawed," she acceded, lowering her head in shame. "I…," she hesitated, afraid to admit the truth. "I thought he was sincere."

Talira closed the gap between them and wrapped her arms around Zuraya. The goddess stiffened, unaccustomed to such physical contact. "Oh, Zuraya," Talira said. "What will you do?"

"The only thing I can do," Zuraya replied, extricating herself from the embrace. She adjusted her glasses, her tone matter of fact as she considered the situation rationally. "The people of Bravneem have been stolen from us. Instead of soaking up their faith, the apostate has somehow relieved them of theirs. That is the only logical explanation for why the city is lost."

She took a deep breath. "And, since I am at least partially responsible, it stands to reason that I should return the city to the fold." She squared her shoulders, nodding at the obvious conclusion. "I will do what the Pantheon demands."

Her hands didn't even tremble as she ushered Talira out the door, her mind abuzz with anticipation.

If Vidhen knew what was good for him, he'd be on his knees, praying – believer or not.

The goddess Zuraya was coming for him.

TOO MANY CLOUDS

The last thing Oronwe remembered from the night before was shrugging out of his soggy coat and tumbling drunkenly into bed. Certainly, he had no recollection of bringing anyone home with him, and yet, through the headache that wailed between his temples like those damned bagpipes his Scottish neighbour insisted on playing at all hours of the night, he heard people talking just outside his room.

Like water flowing upriver, he lumbered into a sitting position, rubbing at his crusty eyes and trying to work some moisture into his dry mouth.

There had been beer, he recalled, and lots of it. The pale stuff they sold here was not as potent as the bitter brew Baba had concocted back home. Warm nights under the African stars, his brothers playing soccer in the dirt, Mama smiling over a steaming bowl of *mieliepap*. The stars here were different. It didn't matter. You hardly ever saw them, anyway. Too many clouds.

He yawned and blinked his eyes a few times.

Cricket. The local university team had won, against the odds. His mates had clapped each other on the back, their elation overflowing like the pints they plied him with afterwards. Something about the rain, and... ducks? He shook his head. The night was a blur of red and green and raucous anthems in a lilting language his ears hadn't grown accustomed to yet. Had there been dragons?

"Focus," Oronwe whispered to himself. There was someone in his apartment - multiple someones from the sound of it - and he was unarmed and in his boxer shorts, the ones he'd bought at the airport that said "I heart Wales".

Also, the room was spinning at an alarming rate.

The voices died down. Oronwe swore under his breath and fumbled under his bed for the squash racket he'd borrowed from a friend last week. It was no *knopkierie*, but it would have to do. His grip was white-knuckled as his bedroom door creaked inwards.

"Ah, you're awake, laddie," said his would-be attacker as he strode into the room.

"About time, too," grumbled the man following on the first's heels. "We thought you were going to sleep the day away."

"Mind you, there's a lot to be said for a good lie-in, but not when you've got company," a third voice piped in. "It's not polite."

Oronwe's brows furrowed. If he'd made a list of things that might kill him one day, lions and hyenas would be on there, maybe a car accident, perhaps trampled by football hooligans. Hell, his great uncle Sipihwo had been struck by lightning on the savannah. But never in his wildest dreams had he imagined three elderly men dressed in red waistcoats and tweed suits to be the end of him.

"Who are you?" he rasped, wondering if he was hungover or hallucinating. Sometimes Baba's beer had made you see things, too.

"O'Reilly, O'Donnell and Maloney at your service, sir," replied the man belonging to the first voice. Wisps of wild red hair framed a face that smiled kindly at Oronwe.

"From the bank of the same name," the second man, O'Donnell presumably, growled. His scowl grooved canyon-like into his face while one of his feet tapped in time to the golden pocket watch he clutched in one hand.

"From Ireland, if that clears things up for you,

laddie," Maloney interjected, tugging on the tip of a bristly white beard that would have done Saint Nic proud.

"It... doesn't," Oronwe replied, resisting the urge to rub at his tired eyes.

"Oh, for the love of Pete!" O'Donnell exclaimed. "Time is money, lad, and we don't have either. Can you help us or not?"

"Money?" Oronwe stammered, wondering who Pete was and how the gentleman's love for him was relevant. He glanced towards his bedside table, where his wallet was clearly visible. "I think I have a tenner or two..."

Maloney guffawed, a tear of laughter rolling down his chubby cheek. "We don't want your small change, lad. We want you to come with us to Dublin. Today, if convenient. Tomorrow, if not."

"Dublin?" Through the fog of his sleep-addled mind, Oronwe tried to make sense of it all and failed miserably.

"Gentlemen," O'Reilly said placidly. "I think what we have here is a case of mistaken identity. The lad doesn't know who we are. Or who he is. Do you, lad?"

Oronwe shook his head. O'Donnell snorted loudly, a sound that reverberated like war drums in Oronwe's beleaguered head.

"I will cut to the chase, then," O'Reilly continued. "Ireland is in the grip of the worst drought the country has seen in twenty years. We haven't had a drop of rain in weeks. That is... problematic... considering our bank cannot operate if we cannot access our funds."

Oronwe's brows knitted even further, to which Maloney responded: "Not a rainbow in sight, my lad."

"You're joking, right?" Oronwo scoffed as the words fought their way into his foggy brain. "Your bank needs a rainbow to operate?"

"Indeed," O'Donnell sneered. "And since you're currently the only rain god in the country, we'd really appreciate it if you can get off your sozzled arse and help us out."

"You will be generously compensated, of course," O'Reilly added.

Oronwe stared at the three men, his mouth hanging open. Laughter bubbled from his lips. "What are you, leprechauns? And you think I'm a rain god? That I control the rain?"

O'Donnell's face turned so red Oronwe suddenly worried about the state of the old man's heart. O'Reilly placed a restraining hand on his colleague's shoulder. His gaze was expectant.

"Wait," Oronwe said, his mirth evaporating like fog before the midday sun. "You're serious?"

This was how he was going to die. Three crazy old men, in his pyjamas.

"Cardiff has seen an unusual amount of rain since you've arrived, lad. It's the only explanation."

"I've heard it blamed on the region's latitude and low air pressure," Oronwe quipped. Laugh in the face of danger, his brother, rest his soul, always used to say.

O'Reilly's face dropped, the hopeful spark fading from his eyes. "So you won't help us?"

Oronwe shrugged. "Sorry, fellas. You've got the wrong guy."

The old man nodded at his companions, his shoulders slumping. The disappointment was plain on Maloney's face and O'Donnell looked like murder on two feet as they filed out of Oronwe's bedroom.

Last to leave, O'Reilly shook his head. "You're wrong, lad," he added, before closing the door behind him.

Oronwe waited until he heard the latch of the front door fall back into place. Then, sighing, he laid down in his bed, his heartbeat fast enough to outrun a cheetah. He closed his eyes and exhaled slowly.

Thunder clapped outside and rain suddenly lashed against his window.

His headache, strangely, was gone.

A WARNING IGNORED

Jenna opened her eyes and coughed, spluttering as she inhaled some of the water threatening to drown her. She was lying on her side in the wet sand, white foam from the gentle breakers lapping against her face. Grimacing, she spat the salty water out and rolled over onto her back. A palm tree swayed in the breeze as she stared at the azure sky above. It took her a moment to remember what had happened.

Mutiny.

She picked herself up from the sand, wincing as she climbed to her feet. The sea must have been rough last night. It felt like she'd been pummelled nearly to death, although she remembered nothing after diving from the plank. Her boots were gone, of course, and so was her hat, but her thick knee-length coat still clung to her wet body. Her breeches and white cotton shirt were caked with sand and scratched unpleasantly against her skin as she stumbled towards the shade of the palm tree.

She smiled when she saw a coconut lying on the ground, and flinched as her bottom lip split. Water. She needed water fast. She smashed the coconut husk open with a large rock, cracked the outer shell and gulped the warm liquid down, rivulets of juice running down the sides of her mouth, and making her hands sticky. The fruit's flesh was bland, but it patched the hole in her rumbling belly.

With her immediate needs satiated, she suddenly remembered why she no longer had a crew.

She stood up and looked about. She knew this beach. She followed the curve of the sand until her eyes could just make out the town walls in the distance, squinting against the morning sun's glare. She'd have to hurry if she hoped to warn them in time.

Jenna hesitated just outside the town gate. Stepping foot inside these walls could spell disaster for her. She glanced towards the ocean, shimmering in the late afternoon glow. Time was limited. She needed to act now.

The guards at the gate stopped her immediately.

"You have some nerve," the first man said as he blocked her way with his musket.

"I need to speak to the Governor. Immediately," Jenna demanded.

"Oh, you'll speak to him, alright," the second guard sneered as he clapped a pair of manacles around her wrists.

Leaving their post unattended, they hauled her off towards the town square, where a large white mansion sat looking out over the bay. Jenna kept her gaze towards the ground, but she heard people whispering her name as the guards bundled her through the large oak doors and up the grand staircase.

A frown creased the Governor's face as he looked up from a stack of papers, annoyed at the interruption. Recognition turned the frown into a scowl.

"I warned you never to come back here."

Jenna wrenched her arms free of her captors' grips and squared her shoulders as she looked into the Governor's eyes. "They're coming."

The man's face paled visibly, and he pressed his lips into a thin line. "And we'll be ready for them. But you brought this upon yourself." He nodded curtly at the guards. The men grabbed her arms again and dragged her from the Governor's office.

A crowd was already gathered in the square, where the gallows waited for her. Jenna lifted her head as the hangman placed the noose around her neck. The sky glowed orange; the sun hanging low over the seemingly blood-red waters of the turbulent ocean waves. In the distance, she could see a black-sailed ship approaching.

She turned towards the Governor, her gaze pleading. "Brother," her lips formed the word, but no sound escaped them.

The Governor averted his gaze and lifted his hand.

HEARTSONG

Skylar wiped her eyes with the back of her hand, trailing snowflakes across her icy cheeks. Cold fingers burned and she looked at them in dismay. Their tips were red and numb.

She was running out of time.

Three days ago, this journey had not seemed so daunting. She'd packed provisions, wrapped herself in thick furs, and waved goodbye to her siblings. If the lines around her mother's eyes had been grooved a little deeper, and if her father's jaw seemed chiselled from granite, Skylar hardly noticed. She had turned her back on her home and their little village and left with a song in her heart.

That song had died when she walked into the snowstorm.

That was when she lost her hat. The frozen stream she tried to cross the next day claimed her backpack, and when the wolves came for her that night, she left everything behind to scale a slippery tree before they satiated their hunger on her flesh. Gloves torn, hair brittle with frozen sweat, tummy growling louder than the beasts prowling below.

For the first time, she missed home. It wasn't the last time.

Somehow, she made it through the night. When she woke the next morning, propped up precariously on a frost-slick bough, the world was shades of grey: charcoal sky above, muddy sludge underfoot, fog all around. It mirrored her mood.

She pressed on. It was tradition, after all.

Skylar blinked. In the distance, cerulean lights

shimmered. Her heart lifted. Trudging turned to shambling. Soon she was trotting. The cobalt lake was within her reach.

The smell stopped her in her tracks. No one had ever warned her that destiny stank of sulphur and rotten eggs.

Scrunching up her nose, Skylar walked up to the lake, footsteps crunching on the obsidian gravel that lined its shore. The water was a milky blue, like the summer sky on a cloudless day. Not a ripple marred its surface. A numinous glow flickered from the deep.

Skylar jumped as a voice cracked the silence apart. "What do you seek, child?"

Her eyes widened as the light broke through the surface and coalesced into human form, a shape with limbs and features like her own, but that was so clearly Other it sent goosebumps rippling down her frozen skin. A creature plucked from bedtime stories stood before her eyes.

The tales were true!

The alfar spoke again, its voice like a rushing waterfall. "Ask your boon."

Skylar paused.

She could count on one hand the names of others who had succeeded before her. Many her age set out in search of answers, but few ever returned, lost in the snow and the wilderness, their names forever haunted their mothers' sad smiles. Those who did return rarely talked about their journey. If they did, you knew their quest had failed.

What should she ask for, she wondered. Wealth? Love? Adventure? Her tongue twisted on all the possibilities.

At last, one word escaped her cracked lips: "Happiness."

A smile crossed the alfar's surreal face. Behind it, the dark sky danced in shades of green and purple. When it spoke again, the alfar's voice murmured like the drip-drip of a spring thaw. "Look within yourself."

The creature faded, the light receded back into the water, and Skylar watched the sky sing.

Then, rubbing warmth back into her arms, she smiled as the song in her heart roared to life again. She turned around, and headed home.

TREE-HUGGER

John's lips curled into a sneer as the night thrummed to life. "Drums," he muttered. "Of course these hippie tree-huggers would have drums."

At least the sound targeted his destination and covered his footfalls. Who knew skulking barefoot through a forest would be so noisy? His tender soles suffered through all manner of crunching sounds: crackling leaves, fallen twigs, rattling stones. He missed his Brunello Cucinellis and his tailored suits. If anyone saw him dressed like this, he'd die of embarrassment.

And this bloody hemp shirt! It made him itch in places he couldn't reach. Probably why these nutters loved their yoga so much. Had to be limber to scratch at all the awkward places.

He peered past the trees. A light flickered ahead, bringing with it the smoky scent of burning pine. "Smart move, dimwits," he growled under his breath. "A bonfire in the woods is always a good idea."

If they burned down this forest, he was going to have a field day in court. It would serve them right. Who did they think they were, with their banners and their slogans and their unkempt hair? They'd cost him millions in PR money already. Who cared about trees anyway? Steel and concrete: that was the future. Not some godforsaken stretch of woods in the middle of nowhere.

He stepped into the clearing just as the drumbeat reached a crescendo. He held his breath, feeling like a sore thumb, but no one paid him any notice. His disguise made it look like he was one of them. Besides, they were busy dancing around the fire like savages, reckless in wild abandon.

He reached for his smartphone. Soon the world would see them for what they were: a bunch of crazies.

The drums stopped.

The dancers stilled.

The fire blazed.

"Impossible," John breathed, dropping his phone to the ground, forgotten.

A woman stepped out of the flames.

She was unlike anyone – or anything – he'd ever seen before. Her ebony skin glowed in the warmth of the fire, and she was dressed in a robe of fluttering butterflies. Magnificent antlers jutted from the waterfall of olive hair that cascaded down her back. When she turned her walnut eyes towards him, John's breath caught in his throat.

Her name rose from every tongue but his, a whisper on the wind. His skin broke into goosebumps.

The woman walked towards him. Where her footprints fell, wildflowers sprung to life, dots of red and blue and yellow on the moss-covered ground. Her scent filled his nostrils as she stopped in front of him, earthy, like freshly tilled soil. Her eyebrows framed a question.

"Who am I, John?" Her voice was terrible, like thunder howling overhead. He dropped his gaze, shaking.

Gently, the woman's touch lifted his chin. His eyes met hers again.

"Say my name."

He swallowed, unable to break her gaze. There was no denying it now. There was no denying *her*. His throat felt like tires on tarmac, but he said it anyway.

"Gaia."

Her lips curled into a smile, and John knew nothing would ever be the same again.

He was one of them now.

HOPE

Judith glanced at her watch as she tumbled out of her car. Traffic from work had been especially hectic that day. Fifteen minutes, that was all she had. No time to park between the lines.

She slammed the door shut and swore quietly as the hem of her floral skirt caught. She opened the door again, releasing the offending garment and grabbing the tattered handbag she'd forgotten in her haste. She pursed her lips at her reflection in the side mirror. People could call them laughter lines all they wanted, it still didn't make her look any younger. She ran a hand through her dishevelled hair, thinking that it was time to redo the roots again. More grey than brown by now. There was just never enough time.

Judith dashed across the parking lot and grabbed the last hand basket as she entered the supermarket. Reciting the list of necessities under her breath, she stepped into the cereal aisle. Daniel wanted chocolate crunchies, but Ashley wouldn't eat anything that wasn't pink and coated in a layer of sugar. And she mustn't forget the bubble gum-flavoured milk, either.

Judith paused as she saw a woman perusing the healthier options, suppressing an envious sigh. Perfectly manicured, perfectly dressed, perfectly composed. The kind of Stepford supermom whose children enjoyed green smoothies and cucumber sandwiches (on rye bread) after winning the 100m butterfly stroke. As if she could hear her thoughts, the woman turned towards Judith and beamed a smile so brilliant at her, Judith wondered if she'd stepped onto the set of a toothpaste commercial. Avoiding eye contact, Judith turned to block Supermom's view of the items she was piling into her basket.

She hurried over to the pasta aisle, where she scooped up two-minute noodles with reckless abandon, until Supermom strolled past with strips of spinach lasagne and bags of fresh tomatoes and basil in her basket. Judith clenched her fist. Could she help it if she just didn't have the energy to cook from scratch?

In the bakery section, Judith bit her lower lip while tucking a loaf of pre-sliced white bread away, watching Supermom scrutinise the whole-wheat and artisanal options on display. She knew her two hooligans would never eat anything that good for them.

By the time Judith had reached the drinks section, she was seriously considering getting herself something a little stronger. Something with a kick, and plenty of it. Instead, she reached for the soda cans stacked onto a pyramid, trying to work out just how much she'd be saving with their discounted price, and watched in wide-eyed horror as the top of the pyramid teetered, then toppled, sending fizzing cans everywhere, crashing down around her feet.

Judith dropped her basket, careless of its contents, and plopped down on the sticky floor. Tears streamed down her cheeks. It was too much. She couldn't do this anymore. She wasn't good enough.

To make matters worse, Supermom was watching her, sympathy written all over her perfect face.

Judith's silent tears turned into gasping sobs.

Then, in a halo of light, Supermom stood in front of her, holding a hand out to her. Wiping the wetness from her cheeks with one palm, Judith took the woman's hand and climbed to her feet, staring at Supermom's shining face, the sound of a thousand angelic voices singing in a choir suddenly echoing inside her skull.

"You're doing the best you can," Supermom said simply.

Judith nodded, vaguely aware of shop employees tidying up behind her. A tingle ran through her arm from the hand of the luminous woman in front of her. For a moment, the world fell away and she floated in a dream of whiteness. A dream where everything was going to be alright. A dream where she was enough. A truthful dream.

Judith was in her car, parked in front of the daycare centre, before the world came back to her. She stared at herself in the rear-view mirror. Nothing had changed.

But everything had changed.

She closed the car door behind her and, with a skip in her step, went to fetch her children.

INCONVENIENT

Rosalyn looked at the dead man lying at her feet. "Well," she said out loud, her voice echoing in the castle's empty hallway. "This is inconvenient."

She lowered her flickering candle closer to the body so she could get a better look. The man's face was peaceful in death; unlined around the eyes, his chiselled jaw a little slack, blond curls framing what one could possibly consider a handsome face. He had broad shoulders tapering down to a lean waist, enveloped within a silk waistcoat and a well-fitted overcoat of purple velvet. A silver sash draped across one shoulder. Powerful leg muscles curved underneath tights tucked into soft leather boots.

"A prince," she sighed. "Not again."

She'd had no peace ever since those two brothers had visited her with their quills and their satchels full of stories. Bored second sons looking for an easy route to a throne assailed her walls constantly now. You'd think brambles with enchanted thorns as thick as her middle finger would deter them, but no, they rose to the challenge. They hacked and hewed her carefully tended plants, and smashed her windows and trod mud all across her carpets.

And then ended up prostrate in her hallway.

A loud snore erupted from the dead man at her feet.

Rosalyn nearly dropped her candle in fright. Heart racing, she prodded the body with one slippered foot. The prince's chest rose and a breath rumbled through his parted lips.

Asleep!

She dropped to her knees and quickly inspected his body. There! A tiny thorn was embedded in the palm of his right hand. Too small to kill.

A tingle ran down Rosalyn's spine as she stared into the man's possibly-handsome face.

Could he be *The One?*

Her eyes were drawn towards his lips, like ants towards a cube of sugar. They looked soft and inviting. She hovered above his face, her lips inches from his, her breath mixing with his.

Then she sat up, shuddering, and pushed herself to her feet. She smoothed the folds of her satin gown straight again.

"Utterly inconvenient," she declared, stepping over his body and continuing on her way.

A Moonlit Night

The forest was unusually dark that night. Arik peered through the shadows, looking for the elusive snowdrop flowers that only bloomed when the twin moons were both full. A double moon night, as he called it, was a very rare occurrence, but he'd kept track of their passage on a carved lintel in his cottage and he'd made his calculations.

And he'd been right. When the light had faded earlier that evening, both heavenly bodies were in the sky, their orbit bringing them inevitably together, like two dancers circling each other in a field of stars.

There! Arik pounced on the delicate little bloom peeking out from the underbrush. He plucked it carefully, almost reverently, and placed it inside the small silver-threaded pouch tied to his waist. Someone had once told Arik that these blooms were tears that had fallen from the sky, tears of joy shed by the twin sisters, Eirlys and Amaris, at being reunited after months apart. Whether that was true or not, Arik didn't know, but the flowers were the most potent cure-all he had ever encountered, and so he came to the forest every double moon in search of them.

Tonight, he searched in vain. A single flower was all he found.

Discouraged, Arik trudged back the way he had come, following the worn footpath through the trees that led to his stone cottage on the edge of the woods. As he walked, his fingers strayed towards the pouch. He would have to use it sparingly and only in great need. There would be no easy relief for simple ailments, not for him nor the villagers who came to him in times of need.

Arik's footsteps ground to a halt as he passed the perimeter of the forest and stared up at the sky.

There was only one moon looming overhead, and it was red as blood.

Movement pulled his attention from the sky. A prone figure lay across the path. It was barely breathing.

Forgetting the ill omen above, Arik hastened towards the figure. He gasped when he drew near. It was a young woman, pale as snow, clad in a simple white dress. A pool of crimson blossomed across her chest. A mortal wound.

She had only one hope.

Arik swooped the woman into his arms and, kicking the door open, carried her into his cottage. He placed her on his bed, heedless of the blood staining the covers. Two steps took him to the silver urn, always filled with fresh water, and he poured some into a wooden bowl. He pulled the snowdrop from the pouch and crushed the entire blossom in his hands before dropping the petals into the water.

Gently, he lifted the woman's head and lowered the bowl to her grey lips. Her eyelids fluttered as Arik helped her swallow the potion, careful not to waste a drop. When the bowl was empty, he placed it on the bedside table and watched as a blush of colour returned to the woman's pallid cheeks.

Slowly, her eyes opened and her gaze rested on Arik's face. He sensed a familiarity in her look, like someone who had spent years watching, finally being seen. It felt as if time stood still, a moment in which the intimate connection of two souls irrevocably drew together.

He sucked in a soft breath as her lips parted in a smile.

"I knew you'd save me." Her whispered words wove around his heart. He knew instantly that he would do anything to keep this woman safe.

"Who are you?" he breathed.

Her eyes were deep pools of light as she held his gaze. "You know."

"Eirlys." The name was honey on his lips. She nodded, sending shivers across his skin. On moonlit nights like these, legends came true, and myths were made flesh.

"Who did this to you?"

"You know that too."

Arik's brows creased into a frown. "Amaris."

Her smile faded as her sister's name hovered between them. Her face hardened with resolve and she clenched her soft hands into fists before pushing herself into a sitting position.

"I did not expect her attack," Eirlys said. "She will not catch me off guard again." Her words were weighted by the implacable determination of a celestial being with the power to shift the tides. Arik shuddered at the cold fury emanating from her.

The sisters' nighttime dance would no longer be joyous. Perhaps it never had been.

Perhaps they had always been at war.

There was blood on the moon that night. Arik knew that if he let Eirlys return to her twin, the future would be bathed in it, in the sky, and perhaps on earth as well. He could not risk it.

He would not risk her.

He placed a hand on her arm, and her gaze whipped back to his.

"Stay," he said.

His heart hammered in his chest as time slowed to a crawl. Now, in this moment, there was only him and only her, and their eyes on each other. No cosmic confrontation, no sibling rivalry, no double moon in the sky. Just a man and a woman, willed together by fate.

At long last, her gaze softened.

THE RETURN

A thousand hearth fires winked at him from the valley below, like stars in the endless sky above.

Regan glared down at his erstwhile home. Ten years. And look how they've grown. Flourished. While he had been banished to walk the wilds, living from hand to mouth, killing to survive, surviving to kill, his little village had grown into a city.

His right hand itched towards the jagged blade strapped to his waist. He longed to hear the rasp of steel on steel, to feel the warm spurt of blood as it ripped through bone and entrails alike, to see the life leaving his enemy's gaze. And he had many enemies down there.

He stepped forward and swore as his body barrelled into the barrier, invisible, yet solid as a stone wall. They had not forgotten about him, either, it would seem.

Time changes everything, and a man does not survive for so long without learning many new skills.

Regan shed his clothes as a snake sheds its skin. Naked, he howled, first in rage, then in pain, as his body contorted. Limbs elongated, claws ripped through fur-covered paws, fangs ruptured from his upper jaw. Where once a man stood, a monstrous mountain lion now prowled the perimeter.

Tentatively, the feline tested the barrier. Nothing. Its lips parted in a snarl. With a powerful leap, the beast jumped through the invisible wall and bounded down the hill.

OCCUPATIONAL HAZARD

T homas was in a bad mood.

I could tell today was not the day to ask for the flash drive he had borrowed by the scowl he wore as he stormed into the office. He was a whirlwind of jacket, scarf, cables and papers as he sat down at his desk and powered on his PC. If his keyboard could complain, it would protest loudly at the abuse it was suffering under Thomas' pounding fingertips.

I watched my colleague closely.

It wasn't often that he came to work looking like a walking death threat. Normally, he was the most jovial person I knew, laughter lines crinkling around his eyes, a witty quip rolling off his tongue, always ready to lighten everyone's mood. If you were feeling under the weather, Thomas was the guy you took a smoke break with.

But on days like these... oh boy. Things happened around Thomas. Strange, inexplicable things.

Like that time we were in the boardroom with an indecisive client. After a marathon seven-hour scoping session that involved endless back and forth arguments between the stakeholders, the client sat back in her chair, sipped leisurely on her tea, and said: "We'll keep it exactly as it is for now."

That tea sloshed all over her expensive suit the next minute and I nearly choked on my bland biscuit as a series of loud thuds rattled the boardroom door. A glance at the vein throbbing angrily at Thomas' temple confirmed my suspicions. Nervously, I walked around the table, wide-eyed gazes following my every move, and opened the door. The kitchen's entire stock of steak knives was embedded in the thick wood.

Needless to say, we didn't get that deal.

Once, when Thomas was on the phone with a particularly challenging end user, the lights in our office started flickering. I heard my colleague grind his teeth as he tried to explain why he couldn't just alter auditable data in the back-end, and the more his temper flared, the more LCD screens started popping and fizzling all around us. By the time he had slammed the phone down, the whole room was filled with smoke and the fire alarm had gone off.

They called it a fluke power flux and blamed it on load shedding. I knew better.

I could almost feel the waves of anger rolling off Thomas now as he paged through a specification document thick enough to be the sole cause of deforestation in the Amazon. His highlighter screeched irritably across the pages. A menacing growl rumbled from his chest as the lady who watered the plant beside his desk accidentally spilled a few drops on his papers. I held my breath as streams of pink ink ran across a technical diagram. The angles on Thomas' face turned so hard you could slice cheese with them.

I stood up. Time to intervene.

Exactly five minutes later, as I strode out of the kitchen with a mug of steaming coffee in my hand, all hell had broken loose.

The plant beside Thomas' desk had grown three times its size and had shot through the ceiling. Vines were creeping across the walls and the paper copier was overrun with a mound of brambles so thick it could hide a sleeping princess. An obscenely large Venus flytrap guarded the door to the boss' office. It snapped at me as I scurried past.

Our office looked like a scene out of *The Day of*

the Triffids.

"Here you go, Thomas," I said, holding the strong black brew out at him. My heart rate shot sky-high as I felt something cold and clammy clamp around my ankle.

Thomas looked up from his paperwork and blinked at me. Wordlessly, he took the cup and placed it against his lips, savouring the rich aroma. His eyes closed as he took a sip, and then breathed out slowly, a sigh of relief.

The thing around my leg let go. The vines along the walls slowly retreated. The plant by Thomas' desk shrunk back to its normal, non-threatening size.

Thomas opened his eyes and smiled at me.

"Thank you. I needed that."

*

PRECIOUS

Keisha scanned the horizon. Nothing but sand and relentless sun as far as the eye could see. Heat waves rolled across the dunes, leaving shimmering trails of cooler air in their wake. A warm gust blew tendrils of black hair across her face and Keisha wiped the strands irritably from her bronze skin. She idly drew a finger across her chapped bottom lip. Perhaps they could spare a swallow of water before the diviner arrived.

Turning her back to the dunes, she stepped from the rocky outcropping on which she had stood watch and walked the few quick strides towards the little pond she had liberated a week ago.

She unhooked the empty flask hanging from the sash tied around her waist and unscrewed the lid. Bending down on one knee, she leaned over and scooped water into the little vessel, careful not to spill any drops onto the desert sand. The water was lukewarm, sun-baked, but it tasted like heaven as the liquid slid down her throat. She licked the last droplets from the lid before replacing it. No point in wasting something so precious.

Keisha resumed her post on the rock. Squinting into the sun, she noticed black dots circling in the sky not too far away. Vultures. They must have found the body. Good.

Her eyes were drawn to a trail of dust muddling the blue expanse in the distance. Finally.

They were moving her way rapidly, much faster than she expected and much faster than a camel was capable of. As the figures drew closer, Keisha loosened the scimitar in the scabbard hanging from her hip. There were too many men in this caravan. She had expected two, at most. She counted five. And they were on horseback.

Steel rasped as Keisha pulled the scimitar loose.

Dust enveloped her as the horses closed in, their riders halting them in a crescent moon around her. Keisha held her breath until the dirt had settled down again. The horses smelled of sweat and fear, the men upon them stank of violence and greed.

"Move aside, woman," one of the men commanded. His voice was harsh and guttural, like the blade of a knife scraping on a whetstone.

"No," Keisha said.

"Move aside or we will ride you down," the man warned. His tone brooked no further argument.

Keisha squared her shoulders and lifted the scimitar threateningly. "If you want it, come and claim it."

She clenched the fist of her free hand. The ground started shaking, sending tremors through the sand. The riders' horses bucked, their eyes rolling wildly, foam flecking their upturned lips. The ground rumbled and a crack in the dry earth erupted under the animals' hooves.

One of the riders, struggling to control his mount, turned towards Keisha, his eyes as large as the full moon. "Demon!" he screamed, pointing at her. He kicked his horse in its side and the animal sped off, away from Keisha. Horses rearing, his companions turned tail and raced after him.

All but the leader fled. In the confusion, the man's horse had thrown him off. He picked himself up, his face a mask of rage. Shouting a wordless battle cry, the brute flung himself at Keisha.

She ducked, rolling to the ground and was back on her feet just in time to parry a swipe from his curved sword. Sparks flew as their weapons met. His sheer strength pushed her to one knee. The man loomed in, his face close enough that she could smell his rancid breath.

"The water is mine, witch," he growled.

Without warning, Keisha pulled back, falling to the ground. The man lost his balance and tumbled after her. She rolled aside just in time, pulling a knife from her boot. The metallic tang of blood filled the air as red liquid squirted from the slit in the thug's throat.

Keisha climbed to her feet and prodded the dying man with her foot. He lay slumped, unmoving. As his eyes glazed over, she turned her back on him and walked towards the pond, wiping her grime-covered knife on her sand-encrusted pants.

She dropped to her knees in front of the water, taking a deep breath. Her hands were shaking.

"You're safe, my friend," she whispered.

The water rippled in the still air. "Thank you," it murmured in response.

SHIRI'S TREASURE

A whip cracked over Shiri's head. She ducked, narrowly missing its sting, and stumbled to the ground, her energy spent. Rivulets of sweat ran down her scarred back, the salty burn an unwelcome companion, but one she had gotten used to by now. The back of her neck, where she had tied her black hair into a scraggly ponytail, burned in the late afternoon sun, red as blood on the horizon.

"Get up!" the slaver shouted, spittle flying everywhere. He hefted the whip again, threateningly.

Shiri flinched in anticipation, but the lash never landed. Another voice said: "Leave her. Plenty more of them around."

Someone kicked her, viciously, and she sprawled down into the dust. Her body refused to get up. She swallowed, gagging as her parched throat crusted with sand. Shiri cringed as the whip cracked again, but someone else cried out this time. Wearily, she lifted her head. Dust billowed as the slaves heaved the enormous block of carved stone forward, inch by inch, the tendons in their half-naked bodies bulging with the strain. In the distance, she could just see the base of the new pyramid ascending from the ground. It would rise taller still, until it peaked with the sun. The god-king demanded higher, better, more than his predecessor, and slaves like her toiled and died until it was done.

Shiri dropped her head to the ground again, closing her eyes in resignation. No more. She'd had enough. Her bones would litter the desert floor, like so many of her people before her, ground to dust by wind and time until she was part of the sand that infested every nook and cranny of this cruel land.

She lay there until the dust had settled, until she could no longer hear the whips crack or the slaves cry out. She lay until the blistering heat faded and her body started shivering, until hunger gnawed at her belly. She lay there, unmoving, until a scratching sound made her open her eyes.

Blinking, her lids crusted with sand, she stared at the crab scuttling across the dune. A memory of home followed in its wake. Of a river, flooding its banks, tall trees swaying overhead, the smiling faces of her siblings as they hunted the thick-shelled crustaceans. Of her mother's hands, strong and sure as she cracked the hard shells open, revealing the treasure inside. Of her father's grin as grease ran down his face while he savoured the tender flesh. Shiri blinked dry tears from her eyes as the memories faded, leaving nothing but sand and sorrow behind.

The flapping of wings filled the air. Shiri lifted her face to a see a crow hovering over the crab. The crustacean hunkered down as the bird pecked at it. She sighed. Like hers, the crab's bones would litter the desert floor tonight. She closed her eyes and waited for the end.

Shiri's eyes fluttered open as a sudden squawk split the night air. She pushed herself to her knees, adrenaline suddenly pumping energy back into her limbs.

The crow was dead. Its neck was snapped, dangling limply from between the crab's pincers. Shiri's eyes widened as she watched the crab tear the bird apart, eagerly devouring its flesh, leaving nothing but a pile of black feathers sticking out in the sand.

Shiri surged to her feet. It was a sign. Her blood boiled with purpose, her heart hammered against her chest. She could see it so clearly in her mind's eye now. The crab was a symbol for her people.

Grabbing a nearby rock, she crushed the crustacean, hearing the hard shell splinter under the weight of her calloused hands. Eagerly, she dug its soft flesh out, feeling her body's energy renewed with every juicy bite. Finally, she licked her fingers clean and dropped the empty shell into the sand.

Her jaw hardened as she gazed at the pile of black feathers, all that was left of the dead crow. Her fists clenched. She lifted her head towards the sun rising red on the horizon. A new dawn.

The time had come.

Soon, the desert sand would be seeped in blood. She was the crab. The crows had better flee.

LISA'S CHOICE

"We're here!" Andrew said as the great wrought-iron gate slowly swung open. The path curved away from it, obscured by a hedge of tall manicured bushes. Carefully tended roses lined the driveway at even intervals.

"Finally," Keri mumbled, while Josh didn't even bother to comment.

Lisa rolled her eyes at the two teenagers in the back of the car. They both had their heads down, engrossed with their phones. She remembered a time when a weekend away had excited the entire family. No one had worried about Wi-Fi access or grumbled about missing out on anything then.

Gravel crunched underneath as the car slowly cornered the bend. Dappled light played across the window as they drove through an avenue lined with tall oak trees. Lisa rolled her window down and breathed deeply. Her heart lifted. The sweet scent of the roses mingled with that of freshly cut grass. A bee buzzed in through the window, looped the interior, and flew out again, intent on its own business.

Lisa followed its bumbling flight until her breath caught in her throat. She gasped as their destination came into view.

A stately manor house stood at the end of the driveway. Ivy climbed across its two-storey redbrick façade, and Lisa counted at least five chimneys poking out from the grey slate roof. Steps led up to a weathered door that had recently been painted white. A brass knocker in the shape of a lion's head guarded the entrance.

"Do you like it?" Andrew asked as the car came to a halt in front of the old building. His eyes were sparkling as Lisa nodded, too excited for words. "And it's entirely ours for the weekend."

"It's perfect," she breathed as she climbed out. Doors slammed as the rest of the family followed her.

Andrew threw his arms into the air, encompassing the manor house and the gardens surrounding it. "Can I deliver the perfect getaway or what?" he exclaimed.

"It's okay." Josh shrugged, pulling his hoodie over his head and holding his phone up for a better signal. Keri was already taking selfies with the house in the background, pouting into her phone's lens for her Instagram followers.

"Grab your luggage," Andrew said, unlocking the trunk. "There's no butler service here." He winked at Lisa as the kids grumbled some more and handed her the key to the front door.

Inside, the house did not disappoint. Floral wallpaper, hardwood floors, cosy furniture. A fireplace crackled softly, filling the room with a comfortable warmth. A grand staircase led upstairs.

The kids were bickering as they lugged their suitcases through the entryway. Ignoring their whining, Lisa skipped up the steps and opened the door leading to the master suite. Her eyes widened and her ears tuned out the noise from below.

An antique wooden dresser stood in the far corner of the bedroom, almost touching the ceiling. Its mahogany panels shone in the light streaming in through the window. Lisa walked towards it as if in a dream, as if it were calling to her. She ran her hand across the pictures engraved into the wood; scenes of frolicking centaurs and wispy nymphs almost coming alive under her touch.

She pulled the doors open. A smile crept across Lisa's face. The dresser was filled with thick fur coats. Whimsically, she stuck her hand in between them and chuckled as she touched the back panel.

"Always worth a try," she murmured to herself as she pulled her hand back.

"Here's your suitcase, love," Andrew said, entering the room in a flurry of bags and coats. He grinned knowingly when he saw her standing in front of the dresser. "Any luck?"

"Not this time," she said, turning towards her husband.

"One day," he promised with a twinkle in his eye. "Settle in so long. I'll take the kids exploring in a minute. The website promised extensive grounds. Apparently, there's a maze and an archery range. That should get them away from their tech for a while."

"One can always hope," Lisa replied, heaving her suitcase onto the bed. "I'll be down in a minute."

Andrew kissed her on the cheek and then headed towards the door. He paused. "Oh, I just remembered. Your Aunt Susan called while I was still outside. Give her a ring, will you?"

"Sure."

An icy wind brushed against Lisa's cheek as Andrew left the room. She turned around, looking for an open window, but both were shut tight. A wisp of hair tickled across her face. She turned towards the still-open closet. Had she just imagined the coats shifting?

"Impossible…" Lisa whispered.

Hesitantly, she stepped closer to investigate. Her hand hovered in front of the coats. A chilly breeze sent goosebumps tingling up her arm. Closing her eyes, she pushed her hand deeper.

Lisa's eyes shot open and she scrambled back from the dresser.

Trembling, she opened her hand and stared at

the clump of snow melting in her palm.

Her head jerked towards the dresser as the faint sound of music drifted from it. Pan flute, if she wasn't mistaken. She took a step closer.

She jumped at Andrew's voice coming from downstairs. "Lisa! Come look! There's a deer grazing by the window!"

Keri's shrill shriek bounced off the walls. "I'll bet it's covered in fleas and lice. Shoo, shoo!"

"Don't be an idiot," Josh piped in. "It looks just like your last boyfriend. Only smarter."

In the bedroom, Lisa hovered, indecisive.

The dresser sang to her.

Below, her family called.

She took a tentative step…

THE BOY

S tars twinkle in the sky as Mara wakes from her dark slumber. Shaking her mane, black as the deepest winter night, her flanks glossy as polished obsidian, she neighs once, a scream that echoes like thunder on a storm-clouded night.

Powerful muscles propel her from her resting place. Like lightning, she flits from one house to the next, visiting homes drenched in darkness, the slow inhale-exhale of slumber the only sound on the still air.

Ever searching, but never finding, she gazes into the hearts of those who lie resting in their beds, looking for a seed of hope, a spark of something pure. Each heart she touches fuels the anger coursing through her veins. Repulsed, Mara flees, leaving fear and horror and tears in her wake.

Until she finds the boy.

Curious, Mara edges closer to the child. Curled up in bed, his arms wrapped around a worn and much-loved stuffed rabbit, blond curls glinting in the moonlight falling in through the window, his face smooth in the untroubled sleep of the very young and the very innocent.

Mara sniffs uncertainly. In his heart she sees cotton candy, and tadpoles, and pirate adventures, and wildflowers for mummy, and fireflies, and skipping stones, and hot cocoa, and yellow balloons, and fuzzy blankets, and long hugs, and summer showers, and muddy puddles, and sandcastles, and bedtime stories, and superhero capes, and squishy pink marshmallows.

Her ears twitch nervously. Her tail swishes hesitantly.

Softly nickering, Mara lays down beside the boy, her head on the pillow beside his, breathing in the soapy-sweet smell of him. She closes her eyes and, the warm breath of the boy mingling with her own, quietly fades away.

And the boy, still asleep, smiles softly.

ACKNOWLEDGEMENTS

This compilation would not be the same without my alpha reader, Schalk van der Merwe, who goes above and beyond the call of duty, dropping everything to help me out of writing slumps, brainstorming outrageously creative ideas to improve my really short short stories, and just generally cheering me on. Every writer needs a buddy like you, buddy!

A special thank you goes out to Gaynor Daly and Christy Courtney, two of my readers who I can always count on to write to me after I've sent out a flash fiction to tell me how much they loved the story. Readers like you make this creative rollercoaster so worthwhile!

As always, thank you to my bestie, Claudette van der Merwe, for cheerleading, chocolate, and copious amounts of cake when I need it most.

And most of all, thank you to my family for their endless support and belief in me. A very special thank you to my mum and dad and my hubby for your continued encouragement. I would never have had the courage to keep on writing, and unleashing these words upon the world, if you hadn't urged me on and supported me every step of the way. Love you!

WANT MORE?

For more titles in the Reverie Flash Fiction series:

SUNEELEROUX.COM/BOOKS/REVERIE-FLASH-FICTION/

If you've enjoyed this book, please consider leaving a review on Goodreads or your platform of choice.

About the Author

Suneé le Roux is a South African author of contemporary and high fantasy stories that blend myth, magic, and adventure. She lives in South Africa with her Welsh husband and their young wizard-in-training.

She loves nothing more than to hear from readers. Connect with her here:

Website: www.suneeleroux.com
Email: contact@suneeleroux.com
Facebook: www.facebook.com/authorsuneeleroux/
Instagram: www.instagram.com/suneeleroux/

WWW.SUNEELEROUX.COM

Read on for an extract from

MYTH
HUNTER
(MYTHICAL MENAGERIE SERIES #1)

BEGINNER'S LUCK

"Shit!" I swore as I stumbled and fell flat on my face.

I lay there for a few seconds, contemplating life, love, the universe and everything else, all the while getting soaked to the bone by the incessant drizzle that had turned the streets of London into a slippery nightmare. It took me a while to realise that both my hands, currently stretched out before me as if in supplication to some uncaring, yet doubtlessly chortling, deity, were touching bits of paper. I clutched onto them as I pushed myself to my feet, ignoring the stares of passersby, none of whom had even the slightest decency to offer a hand.

In my right hand was some kind of wanted advert. I scrunched it up and pushed it into the pocket of my tweed jacket.

Of more interest was what I held in my left hand. A fifty-pound note! I stared at it dumbly, numbly, not believing my luck. A stupid smile crept across my face. I got to eat steak tonight!

That smile twisted into a scowl when I saw the reason for my fall. The sole on the right foot of my best pair of loafers gaped wide open. My sock was sticking out. Not exactly the impression I wanted to make at tomorrow's interview. Not that it would make any difference, I imagine. I could show up in a suit made of hundred-pound notes and I would still not get the job. The financial world was unforgiving, especially if you'd made the sort of mistake I had made.

Still, I had to try. Giving up meant not eating, and forfeiting on this month's rent. And, worst of all, having to listen to yet another one of Mother's tirades.

I surveyed my surroundings, trying to get my bearings again while absentmindedly scratching my stubbly chin. I had just crossed Westminster Bridge on my way home from an interview in the South Bank. Big Ben towered over me, like some giant from myth; silent, judgmental, implacable. Both tourists and Londoners swarmed past me, indifferent to just one more well-dressed twenty-something hoping to somehow survive in this pitiless city.

I squinted as a trickle of water dribbled from my sandy blond hair into my eyes. A rainbow arched over the Houses of Parliament and descended towards the Tube station where the sign for a shoe repair shop caught my eye. I pulled my jacket closer about myself and hurried towards it.

A bell jingled as I walked through the door, the strong odour of shoe polish and sweaty feet assaulting my nose. A man slightly older than me looked up from behind the counter where he was busy repairing someone's footwear. His red hair blazed like a furnace in the darkness of the tiny, windowless shop, reflecting the light from a single spotlight that provided just enough illumination for him to work by. An easy smile crossed his freckled face, blue eyes twinkling with merriment as he greeted me with a distinct Irish lilt.

"What can I do for you?"

I pointed at my offending shoe. "Think you can fix this?"

The man held out his hand and I passed him the shoe, feeling ridiculous standing there in my slightly soggy sock. He stroked his short-cropped beard thoughtfully as he inspected the grinning sole. "Expensive brand," he noted. "You really should take better care of these."

"Can you save it?" I asked, knowing full well I couldn't afford to replace it.

"Sure," the redhead said. "Ten pounds. Come back tomorrow."

"Tomorrow? You want me to walk home barefoot in the rain?" I asked, looking pointedly towards the door where the inlaid glass had steamed up, obscuring the view outside.

The man shrugged.

"Look," I said. "I need that shoe. Is there any way you can fix it now?"

"Sorry, mate," he replied, nodding at the pile of shoes lying on the countertop already. "Got a bit of a backlog here. But..." He reached below the counter and pulled out a pair of white trainers with a green four-leaved clover embellishment adorning the sides.

"My own design," the shoemaker said proudly.

"How much?" I asked. Unfortunately, the days where I refused to wear anything that wasn't a high street brand were long gone.

"Twenty quid."

I sighed. Those fifty pounds were dwindling fast. I handed the note over and sat down to try the trainers on.

"What name should I put on your slip?" the man asked as I tied the shoelaces.

"Ambrose Davids."

"That's... unusual," he said diplomatically.

"You can thank my mother for that," I replied, taking a few steps in my new trainers. They did fit remarkably well. Not particularly stylish, and paired with my brown tweed suit downright ridiculous, but they would have to do for now.

He handed me my change and the slip.

"Thanks," I said in way of farewell. I opened the door and stepped out of his shop.

Thankfully, the rain had stopped, replaced by a

bitingly icy wind. I thrust my hands into my pockets and remembered the other piece of paper I had picked up earlier as my fingers brushed across it. I pulled it out and stared at it.

Instead of the wanted ad I had first assumed, it was a flyer promoting an information session for jobseekers. No further details, just the location, date and time. I looked at my watch and swore again. The session was in fifteen minutes, and about a mile from here. Heedless of the stares once again directed my way, I set out at a jog.

The easiest route was through St James' Park. Ducks quacked as I ran past, dodging pedestrians and cyclists alike. I was out of breath by the time I sprinted past the old war memorial on Waterloo and dripping with sweat when I finally reached Piccadilly Circus, barely sparing a glance for the statue of Anteros and the crowd of camera-wielding tourists around it. By the time I found the unobtrusive door of the venue hidden in a side street, I was already ten minutes late.

The door clicked open when I pressed the buzzer, revealing an empty landing area and a narrow staircase. I took the stairs up two at a time and entered a darkened room on the second floor where a dozen or so people were already watching a slide show. I sat down in the back row, waving apologetically at the presenter in the front as she continued talking.

The woman looked to be in her early twenties too, with dark chocolate skin and a waterfall of black curls framing her face. Her accent was as English as my own, but the African-print scarf wrapped around her throat hinted at a more exotic background.

"As you can see," she was saying, "we are interested in creatures of a more... shall we say, unusual... reputation." She pointed at the screen where a picture of a winged horse on an old Grecian vase was displayed. "We specialise in animals of myth, folklore and fantasy. Your job would be to locate and acquire these creatures on our behalf. This does not come without an element of danger, but you will be handsomely compensated for any risks you may need to take. All we ask is that you deliver the creatures into our care alive and unharmed. Any questions?"

"Yeah." The guy in front of me raised his hand. "What have you been smoking, lady?"

I glanced at the faces around me as laughter bubbled throughout the room. Almost everyone looked sceptical, some shaking their heads in amusement, others frowning in annoyance. One or two even glanced at their watches, barely bothering to hide their yawns.

"I assure you, we are not crazy. These creatures may be scarce, but they are as real as you and I." The presenter looked calmly at the sea of disbelieving faces staring at her. "And they are in danger. They need to be protected."

The man scoffed again, turning an incredulous gaze at the surrounding people. "Is she serious?" he asked of the room. He picked up his coat and stood up. "I'm out of here, lady. Thanks for the fairy tale, but I have mouths to feed. I wouldn't want to send my children off to find the gingerbread house in the woods." More laughter followed as he strode out of the room. One by one, the rest of the people stood up and left, too.

"What a waste of time," a woman said to her friend as they shuffled past me.

The presenter made no move to stop them, but her shoulders slumped a little as she bent over her laptop and turned the presentation off. She flicked a switch on the wall, bathing the room in fluorescent light. Her eyes widened when she saw me still sitting in my chair.

"Was there something?" she asked, a small frown

creasing her forehead.

I stood up, not sure how to explain to her I was desperate enough to go in search of fairy tales if it meant I could eat something other than dry bread the rest of this week. Hell, for a small stipend I would swim the length of the Thames in search of selkies or whatever imaginary creature they wanted right now, no matter if I ended up on Sky News tonight.

"Well, uh..." I hesitated as her brown eyes met my own. She looked me over with one eyebrow raised quizzically. I must look a mess, I realised, all sweaty from the jog here and wearing a water-stained suit. I ran a hand self-consciously through my windblown hair.

"I like your shoes," she said, a small smile playing across her lips. She held her right hand out and I shook it automatically. "Amari Kerubo of the CPPCC. And you are?"

"Ambrose Davids," I replied. CPPCC? Sounded like a remnant of the old Soviet Union. Father would have been looking for conspiracy theories right about now. He'd always had an active imagination.

"Well, Mister Davids," Amari said as she reached into her laptop bag and pulled something out of a side pocket. "I sense you are not quite as sceptical as the rest, so I will give you this." She placed a silver whistle in my hand. "Blow it when you have something we might find interesting."

I stared at the whistle. She had to be kidding me. I suddenly wondered if there was a hidden camera somewhere and my sister would soon show all her friends on YouTube how her brother had fallen for some obscure practical joke.

I looked back at the woman. She raised an eyebrow at me again. I mumbled my thanks and shoved the whistle deep into my pocket, wondering how much I'd be able to flog it for. Without another word, I turned around and left too. This really had been a waste of time.

With twenty quid in my pocket, there would be no eating steak tonight, I thought gloomily as I made my way home on foot. I stopped at a hole-in-the-wall fish and chips shop in Mayfair and ate the greasy fare while walking. I could probably have afforded to take the Tube, but I didn't want to waste the money. No idea when I would get more. Besides, I enjoyed walking, especially now that the rain had cleared up and the wind had died down. Also, I had to admit that these trainers were exceptionally comfortable. At least that was twenty quid well spent.

The light was fading by the time I entered Hyde Park. There were shorter routes home, but I always walked through the park when I had the chance. Something about the trees and the smell of wet grass. It cleared my head.

It was becoming all too apparent that this job interviewing business was not going well. I'm not even sure why they had called me in this morning. They had hardly asked me any questions. Only the one, really - how? How had I made such a crucial mistake? I had shrugged and given them a non-committal answer. The truth would have been too embarrassing, especially in that sterile white boardroom in front of a panel of black-suited and stern-faced brokers.

The sound of a large splash drew me out of my reverie and I stopped short, surprised. I had crossed over into Kensington Gardens and was walking along the path parallel to that part of the Serpentine known as the Long Water. Bushes obscured my view of the lake and I held my breath as I strained to hear what was going on.

Another splash. It sounded too big to be a water bird, and it was too cold and dark for some nutcase in a swimsuit to be out. Gripped by curiosity, I scaled the low fence and pushed past the greenery. My eyes were drawn immediately to a pale figure in the water.

A young woman was floating on her back in the middle of the lake. Her face was pallid under the light of the full moon and her long white dress billowed around her motionless body.

"Help!" I shouted, looking around to see if there was anyone about. Not a soul in sight.

I hesitated at the water's edge. It had never occurred to me that knowing how to swim might one day be a necessary skill. The girl floated, pale and unreachable, like some morbid Lady of the Lake, and me, Arthur, building up the courage to jump in and rescue her.

"Did you off her, then?" a voice behind me said and I nearly jumped out of my skin.

I spun around. It was a teenager, his hoodie pulled low over his eyes so I couldn't make out his entire face, hands thrust deep into his pockets. Probably came here to smoke a joint where no one would see him.

"No, I did not off her," I replied irritably.

"Better call the cops then." He shrugged and turned around, heading towards the path again.

"Hey, wait," I called. "Can you swim?"

"That water looks freezing." He disappeared behind the bushes without a backward glance.

"Unbelievable," I muttered, shaking my head in the direction in which he had left. Then, remembering the need for urgency, I pulled my mobile from my jacket pocket. I dialled Emergency Services and explained the situation. When I ended the call, I turned towards the lake again.

The girl was gone.

Find the full novel here:

BOOKS2READ.COM/MYTHHUNTER